With love to Seamus—C.D.

For my best friend, Mario—J.C.

Designed by Tony Fejeran

Copyright © 2012 Disney/Pixar. All rights reserved. Published by Disney Press, an imprint of
Disney Book Group. No part of this book may be reproduced or transmitted in any form or by any means,
electronic or mechanical, including photocopying, recording, or by any information storage and retrieval system,
without written permission from the publisher. For information address Disney Press, 114 Fifth Avenue,
New York, New York 10011-5690. Printed in the United States of America.

First Edition

1 3 5 7 9 10 8 6 4 2

Library of Congress Catalog Card Number: 2012939977

F322-8368-0-12259

ISBN 978-1-4231-6818-8

Visit www.disneybooks.com

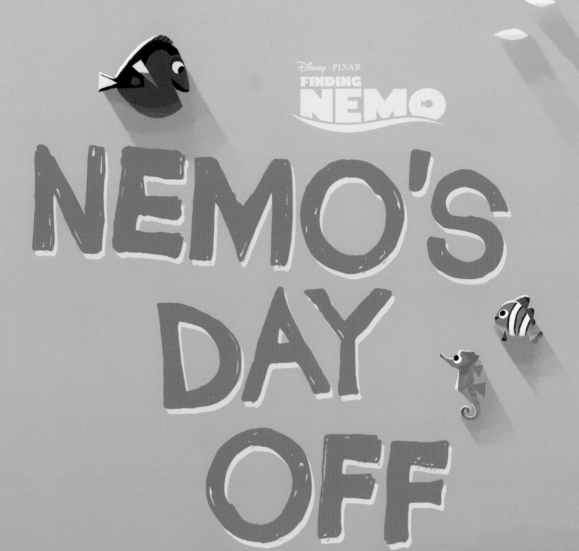

FINDING NEMO

NEMO'S DAY OFF

By Catherine R. Daly

Illustrated by Joey Chou

Disney PRESS

New York

Nemo liked his friends.
He liked having fun.
And most of all, he liked trying new things.

But there was one thing he didn't like—**rules**.
He thought his dad, Marlin, had way too many.

Don't play outside of the neighborhood.

Never have more than one after-school snack.

Rule 3

Do your homework as soon as you can.

Rule 4

Go to bed at a reasonable hour every night.

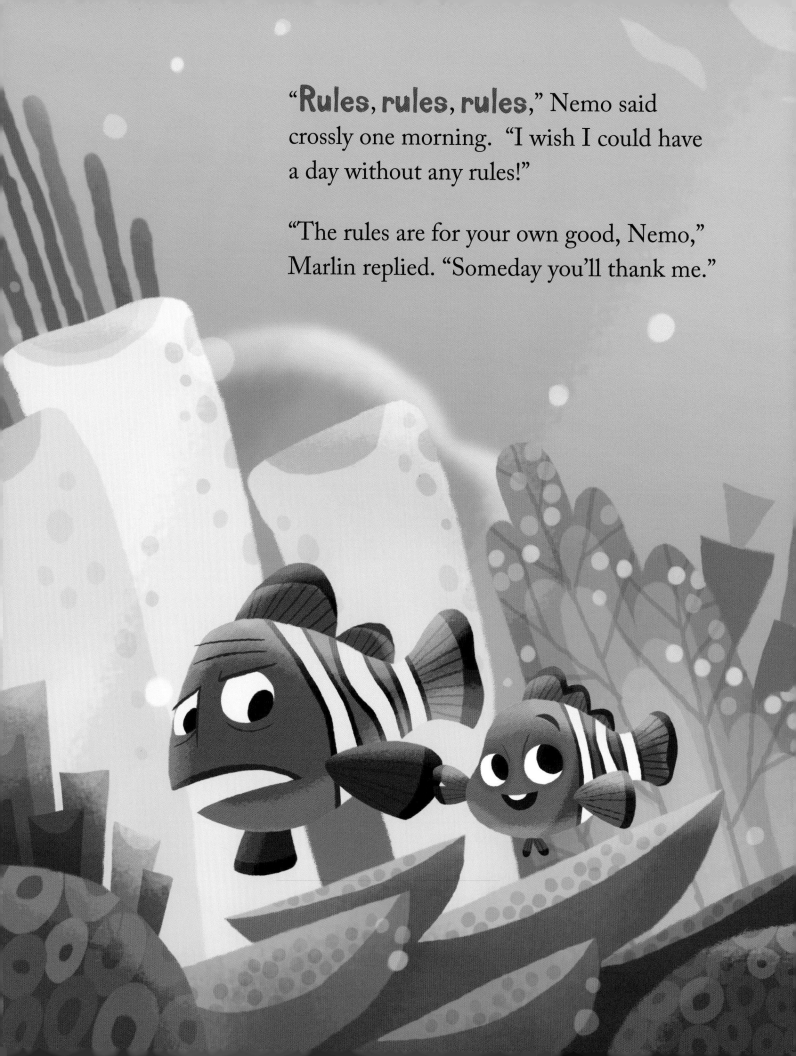

"Rules, rules, rules," Nemo said crossly one morning. "I wish I could have a day without any rules!"

"The rules are for your own good, Nemo," Marlin replied. "Someday you'll thank me."

Just then, Dory swam up.
"Hey, Chico,"
she said.

Nemo liked Dory. She was kind,
fun, adventurous—and very forgetful.

Marlin had an idea.
"Son, I have to go on a little trip.
Dory is going to babysit you."

"I am?"

"You are."

After school, Nemo told his friend Sheldon.

"Dory can't remember anything!" Sheldon replied.

"This means no rules!"

"Hey, Dory!" Sheldon said. "My friends and I are going to go over to the coral reef to play **hide-and-seek**. Can Nemo come?"

"Sounds like fun!" Dory said cheerfully. And that is how Nemo began breaking Marlin's rules.

Nemo ducked in and out of hiding places.

He was having the best time until . . .

. . . he tried to hide in a grumpy moray eel's home and bumped into some fire coral.

Ouch!

"Well, that was exciting!" said Dory. "I've never met a moray eel before. Not as friendly as I expected."

After everyone left, Dory gave
Nemo and Sheldon their
after-school snack.

"How about some
plankton pizzas?"

"All right!"
they shouted.

"You boys haven't had your after-school snack yet!" Dory exclaimed a few minutes later. "How about some **seaweed sandwiches**?"

"You boys haven't had your after-school snack!" Dory squealed. "How about some **kelp cookies**?"

"You boys haven't had your after-school snack!" called Dory. "How about some **sea-grass smoothies**?"

It was getting late. Normally Nemo would be doing his homework.

"Oh!" Dory said. "I just remembered something. I think it's time to . . ."

". . . play **Kick the Clam!**"
said Sheldon, thinking quickly.

"Yes," said Dory.
"That must be it!"

"Now I think it's time to . . ." Dory began.
". . . play **Splash Tag** with Bruce!"
Nemo suggested.

When Bruce said good-bye, Dory remembered something. "Now I am pretty sure it is time to . . ."

"You're right!" said Sheldon.
"It *is* time to play **Dodgecoral**."

"Actually," said Dory, "I am pretty sure it is time to . . ."

Nemo and Sheldon looked at each other. They had run out of ideas.

". . . play **Toss the Sea Disc!**" shouted Dory. "Hey, this is fun. I wish I had thought of it!"

A few hours later, Nemo was ready to go home.

But Dory was having too much fun.
"Think fast,
Harpo!"

Nemo was so tired he didn't catch the sea disc.
Mrs. Puffer's sea-fan curtains were ruined.

Riiip!

"Sorry, Mrs. Puffer." Nemo felt terrible. "I think it's time to go home for real," he told Dory.

She frowned.
"All right, Dino. If you say so."

Nemo was very, very sleepy by the time they got home.

"Well, I guess it's time for bed," he said with a yawn.

"Good night!"

"**Five more minutes!**"
Dory begged.

Nemo shook his head.
"No, Dory, I need to go to sleep."

"Just five more minutes?" Dory asked again.

"Please?"

"Nope, it's one of the rules. And sometimes we have to stick to them. You'll feel better in the morning. Trust me," said Nemo.

Marlin smiled.
"You sound just like me."

"Daddy, I'm so glad you're home!" Nemo cried.
He paused. "Maybe rules aren't so bad after all."

"Well, thanks for everything, Dory," said Marlin.

"You're welcome," Dory replied. "I had a great time babysitting little Fabio." She paused for a moment.

"Or at least I think I did!"